# Father Goose

# & His Goslings

By Bill Lishman

Illustrated by Jack McMaster

ISBN 0-9623072-8-9

Published by Storytellers Ink
Seattle, Washington

Printed in the United States of America

# *Dedication*

To the incredible birds in our world.

Other books by Storytellers Ink:


Beautiful Joe

Black Beauty

Kitty the Raccoon

Lobo the Wolf

The Pacing Mustang

Cousin Charlie the Crow

Sandy of Laguna

The Living Mountain

William's Story

If a Seahorse Wore a Saddle

The Lost & Found Puppy

I Thought I Heard a Tiger Roar

The Blue Kangaroo

# CONTENTS

# Chapter I

## The Dream

The first one just flipped over. It had taken only a tiny ripple in the stream to swamp my leaf and twig boat. My first design might have cost the life of the entire crew of three carpenter ants I had planned to put on board. Only at the last minute had I decided that a test run was necessary first.

Now I knew what had gone wrong. The leaf had been too small and could be overturned by the slightest ripple. This time I chose a bigger leaf and with crew aboard launched the little vessel and followed it along the bank.

The boat sailed smoothly on the surface of the stream, while below it, a school of silver minnows, the size of whales in comparison to the tiny crew, darted away from the bank in perfect unison.

I imagined that I was one of the ants or a miniature Huck Finn rafting down the Mississippi, or maybe the captain of a pirate ship escaping out to sea.

The boat sailed out into the pond my father had created by damming up the stream that ran through our property, and I wished I could have the view the little crew had, drifting slowly over the water, able to peer down into its depths, moving quietly enough so as not to scare away any of the sea life that were down there.

As I scrambled along the bank I realized that all the birds and fish close by were too wary to wait for me to catch up with them and, as the current took my crew far out into the pond, I knew what my next project would have to be. I needed a boat big enough for me.

On a farm, there's always a lot of interesting stuff lying around, and with a little imagination, almost anything is possible. The railroad ties and fence posts I found weren't meant for sailing, neither was the bailing wire I used to bind them together, nor was the design much more sophisticated than my leaf and twig boat. It occurred to me that most people would call my creation a raft, not a boat, but I knew it would be perfect for my next adventure.

Before daybreak the next morning I dragged my boat down to the water's edge for launching. Fog hung low over the fields and pond and a few stars were still visible. I needed to start before first light because chores began very early on the farm, and I wanted as much time as possible for my project. I knew from my mom that the birds would be feeding in the fields even before my father started to work at dawn, and they would soon come to the pond, some to drink, some to swim, some to fish. I wanted to be there first to watch as they arrived.

I pushed the raft into the water as carefully as I could, trying not to disturb the still surface. Staying hidden was important too, so I poled the raft over into the tall reeds, but close enough to the edge to see the whole pond.

As the raft settled, I concentrated on listening. The quiet was broken first by the deep *garumph* of a bull frog. Then one creature after another tuned in until the air was filled with the sounds of the pond coming to life.

The frogs, songbirds and crickets kept up a constant melody, as busy as our local village on market day. Fish jumped out of the water, feeding on insects that skimmed the surface of the pond. Suddenly, a kingfisher slashed through the orange sky from behind me, in a power dive that was certain to bring it crashing into the pond, but at the last moment, in a movement almost too quick to see, it turned back toward the sky, its wings beating, a silver fish squiggling in its beak.

As the sun appeared over the hills, a squadron of mallard ducks dropped out of the sky, quacking happily to each other as the whole group started to land. Just before the first of them splashed onto the pond, a snapping turtle slid off its rock perch into the murky water thoroughly startling me. I recovered quickly, not so the ducks. The whole flock instantly veered off, gaining altitude, to take another look.

I remained perfectly still and, after some circling, one by one they plopped back down onto the pond.

That's when I noticed the blue Heron. It came in on huge quiet wings settling onto the water without a sound. It stood so still that if I had not seen it land I might not have noticed it there.

It stood on stick-like legs, not making a ripple, its sharp bill a spear. As soon as a minnow swam into range, the Heron's head flashed lightning quick into the water, and in an instant the little fish was part of its breakfast.

Over the noise of the ducks as they splashed and frolicked, from far away came a honking sound that attracted my attention. Looking up high in the sky I strained to see what might be approaching next. Eventually I could make out the tiny specks of Canada geese flying in perfect V formation.

What a beautiful sight! Their flight was controlled, ordered, each goose nicely tucked into place to make their group flight as efficient as possible. I tried to mimic their call hoping they would come down and land on the pond, but they paid no attention to my feeble attempts and continued their flight overhead.

Forgetting the pond for a moment I became lost in imagining how our farm looked from so high up, and I tried to picture where the geese were going and how they knew how to get there. Suddenly my day-dreaming was interrupted by my father's voice. "Bill!"

Oh oh! In my bird watching I had lost all track of time. When I stood up to answer, it seemed as if the whole pond lifted up into the sky.

"Coming Dad!"

"Your chores aren't done." I jumped off the raft and joined my dad, getting a soaked foot in the process.

"Where are they going, Dad?" I asked pointing at the geese.

"They're migrating south for the winter, probably heading some-where along the coast of the United States or Mexico. They'll be back again next spring. But never mind that, your calves are hungry and Mike and John are here to see you, but no playing now until all your chores are finished."

"It must be great to fly anywhere you want to go. I wish I could fly with them."

"Guess everybody does when they're young. But every creature is different from the next. We're just not one of the animals that is designed to experience the feeling of free flight."

"I sure would like to."

"Dreaming's fine, Bill, as long as the calves get fed," and he disappeared into the barn.

Mike and John caught up with me, and I thought that if they wanted to try out my raft, they might help me with the chores.

"It's amazing to watch those birds fly. I think flying would be the most incredible feeling in the world," I told my buddies.

"You'd look crazy with wings." Mike kidded me.

"Let's feed the calves," I countered.

Just then Whitey, one of the farm geese that was part of the flock my family kept, came running down the barn ramp in her daily attempt to fly, furiously flapping her wings, teetering through the pear orchard about three feet off the ground, heading toward the pond. She splash-crash-landed into the water with the tumbling grace of a large rock.

"There you go, Bill. Some things are just not meant to fly. And she even has wings!" John said.

Mike laughed. "Did you see that landing? What a dumb goose!"

Mom, hearing this from the back kitchen, spoke up. "Now boys, don't judge something you don't understand. I've seen each of you do some pretty dumb things occasionally, but I know you're not stupid."

"Aw, Whitey just feels like she's one of the wild geese and wants to join them, and I don't blame her," I said, "because I wish I could join them too."

## Chapter II

## Learning Indoors and Out

When our teacher, Mrs. Hood, left the room, John pulled out his latest paper airplane. I tore a page from my notebook and carefully folded the new design that dad had shown me the night before. On a silent count of three, we both sent them flying. Then all the other kids started folding planes. For every kid in the class, there was a different looking plane. When everyone was ready, I started the count.

"Ready ... set ... go!" No sooner had the classroom filled with flying paper, than Mrs. Hood walked in. Stopping short as paper airplanes circled around her, with hands on her hips, she glared at John and me.

"William and John, come here please." We looked at each other and slowly shuffled toward her desk.

"You boys seem to be expert with these paper airplanes, perhaps you can show the rest of the class what makes your planes stay up so long. Now class, everyone put away your books. These two would-be flyers are going to help us design the perfect glider."

The world was a strange place, full of surprises. Just when you think you're in trouble, you end up learning something.

On the walk home through the fields and orchards that day, John and I were feeling particularly good, maybe a bit lucky. We picked a few apples and ate them, then collected some cherries and elderberries from the fence row to bring home.

We played on the old fence my great grandfather had made out of massive tree stumps tipped on their sides. Their gnarled and tangled roots were fun to climb and explore.

As we played, I realized that they were bigger than any of the other forest trees that still grew nearby.

"I wonder how big these trees were?" I asked John.

"Too big to climb, probably."

"I'll bet it was cool when these trees were alive." John was climbing down the other side, and I knew he was headed for the fox den I had found the year before underneath one of the stumps.

"There's nobody home. I wish they were still around," he said.

I waited above the stump, and a praying mantis crawled onto my hand. Turning its triangular head, it stared me in the eye.

When I got home, I asked my mom if she thought the foxes would come back to the den in the stump fence.

"Maybe. But they probably know you found their home, and moved to a safer location."

"But I wouldn't hurt 'em."

"Well, maybe they know that, and maybe they don't."

"What do you mean?"

"Take that stump fence where you found their den. For hundreds of years it was part of a giant forest of cedar and pine. But when your great grandfather moved here, he had to cut down a lot of those trees on our property to grow food, build his home, and keep everybody warm in winter.

"A lot of the animals moved further into the forest. Some got used to living pretty close to people, and were able to adapt. But other animals began to slowly disappear, some became endangered species, or worse, extinct."

"Extinct? You mean like dinosaurs?"

"Like dinosaurs."

"Is the fox almost extinct?"

"I don't think so. They're very smart. Too smart to live in a den that a bunch of little boys have found. The Whooping Crane and the Trumpeter Swan are almost extinct though. We should be taking special care of them. And that means protecting the forests and the land and the water where they need to live."

"But swans don't live in trees."

"No, they don't. But everything in nature is connected, Bill. When one animal or a part of the forest or river changes, it affects all the rest in some way. The swans were hunted for their quills and warm down feathers. That's forbidden now, so maybe there can still be a happy ending to their story."

I was horrified to think that such a beautiful creature might not survive because of humankind, and resolved to think of some way I could help.

## Chapter III

## Mechanical Things

CLINK Clink clink — the pebble rattled around in the bottom of the pop bottle. I must have been very young, but I remember that gravel pile out near our barn. It was as much fun as any toy I've ever had. I tested the sound of a pebble dropping in a tin can. Clang. A single stone tossed into a mud puddle made a perfect little 'plop,' while a handful sounded like popping corn.

My dad's old tractor, a heavy square-looking monster with huge spiked iron wheels and an exhaust pipe that stuck out on the side, was parked next to the gravel pile. I climbed up and dropped a pebble into the rusty pipe, and after what seemed like a long time, a deep *'pang'* rang from inside.

The next day when I went out to play, Dad, oil and grease to his elbows, called me over. "Bill, the tractor's making a strange sound when I start the engine, so I'm taking it apart to find out what's wrong. You can help and I'll explain how it works." I went, not realizing until years later that it had been the pebble I dropped into the muffler that had made that strange rattling sound when the engine was started.

While my mother loved all things in nature, my father loved all things mechanical. He really liked to take apart, inspect, fix, and put things back together again. He knew a lot and could easily explain to me how things worked.

This was my first lesson in the operation of the internal combustion engine. Like anything you don't understand, it seemed very mysterious at first. It wasn't long, though, until I would know enough to fix things myself.

When my dad finished, he straightened up and smiled. "Every time I get mad at this tractor for breaking down, I think about your grandfather who plowed these fields with a team of horses. Fixing a tractor doesn't seem like too much work compared to that."

"What's wrong with using horses, Dad?"

"Nothing's wrong with it. But look at this sign." He pointed to where it read: 40 HP. "That means horse power; this engine can pull the plow with the strength of forty horses."

"Wow, imagine forty horses trying to pull one little plow."

"Now, the job gets done much faster so we have more time for other things, like enjoying your mom's rhubarb pie. Come on."

## Chapter IV

## Flying Machines

My parent's interests, nature and technology, helped shape my life and career. My love for mechanical things led me to spend many hours in a welding shop learning the craft of forging and welding metals. Eventually this gave me the skills to express myself creatively. Sculpting nature's birds and animals of all sorts became my profession. The more I learned, the more I enjoyed myself.

Much later, after I had a family and some land of my own, something unexpected happened that would change my life.

My friend Mike, who so many years before had made fun of my desire to fly with the birds, called one day full of enthusiasm, so much so, he was nearly shouting over the phone, "Bill, I've got a hang glider! It's the latest thing. Come over and check it out!"

It didn't take me long to get there. My interest in flying had never died, and though Mike and I had many long talks about flying machines and how we might create one that could fly like a bird, this was the first real step in that direction.

When I arrived, Mike explained how the hang glider was constructed and how it worked, then he flew gracefully off a small knoll a few times. My palms sweated as I waited my turn.

I climbed only halfway up the hill before taking off. My flight was short but thrilling and this moment of excitement was enough to convince me. "I've got to build one of my own!"

Mike said: "I need some help making a special drilling jig. Let's do an energy exchange; give me a hand with the jig and I'll help you build a hang glider." And that's just what we did.

Before long my very own glider was ready to fly. Standing on the knoll on a day when the breeze was light, the sun shining, and my knees weak with nervous excitement, I gathered up my courage and started running down the hill. The air rushing over the wings gently lifted me off the ground, and there I was finally gliding on wings of my own making.

My flight didn't last long. Airborne for only a few seconds, I came stumbling down, my landing almost as bad as the ones our goose Whitey used to make into the pond. There were many, many practice flights before I was able to stay in the air and a lot of bumps and bruises before my landings smoothed out. Flying wasn't simple or magical. It was a combination of correct design, technique and skill, something that had to be learned, and though it was a little slow and painful, I did get better at it.

"Do you feel like a bird in that glider yet?" Mike asked one day.

"Sort of. But not really so smooth—or effortless."

A few days later I saw a news story on television which helped us solve this problem. In California, another flyer had introduced a newly styled glider, the Icarus. The news cameras showed pilots launching themselves high over ocean cliffs where the strong updrafts, the new design and a lot of skill made it possible for the flyers to stay in the air for as long as five hours!

I saved my money to buy one, but by that time, nine months later, someone had taken the idea even further, and added an engine to the glider, calling it the Easy Riser.

It was a noisy little craft, but there would be no more tiresome carrying of the glider back up the hill, and the flights could stretch to hours rather than seconds.

This flying machine, no longer just a glider, promised even greater freedom in the air. I was very excited to try it. When I did, it was another learning adventure, which cost me a few bent wings and two additional years of hard work.

That was only the beginning. In the years that followed I rebuilt my machine many times, until it evolved into a very refined little airplane. Rather than being confined in a cockpit, I was surrounded by air, experiencing maybe the closest sensation one could ever have of a bird's free flight. Sitting between the wings, goggles on tight, I could cruise at the same speed as the migratory birds, anywhere between twenty-five and forty-five miles per hour.

Using meager funds, a lot of muscle and the help of friends, I built a hangar and created a six hundred foot airstrip behind our house. We christened the hangar, "Purple Hill Aerodrome," in honor of the purple flowers that bloomed along the runway.

In the calm of morning or evening I could be airborne in short order, soaring over the local countryside, enjoying the beautiful colors of each changing season, and watching the flocks of birds from this whole new vantage point. With the speed and agility of the little plane I had hoped to be able to fly with the birds, and there was nothing to keep them from flying close to me if they were the least bit curious. But none were. The birds wouldn't come near me.

In fact, the opposite happened. Just like my raft on the pond, whenever I got near any birds they promptly veered away in the opposite direction. The noise of the engine must have frightened them and they stayed very clear of this unknown object.

It finally dawned on me that if I was going to fly with the birds we were going to have to get to know each other better.

But how? I thought about the problem for weeks.

As I was pondering these thoughts, disaster struck. In a huge snow storm, my makeshift hangar collapsed, completely crushing the little plane inside. I replaced it eventually with another ultralight aircraft, called a Lazair.

## Chapter V

## A Breakthrough

It's strange sometimes how things that seem very far apart, end up connecting, coming together. My work as an artist brought a new job my way, designing sets for a nature film for the IMAX theaters. To gain background for this new venture, I wanted to see the IMAX film, "Skyward," so one evening I collected the family and headed for Toronto.

The movie was really exciting. The screen was so large and the picture so clear, that I had the amazing sensation of actually being right there in the film myself. What really impressed and surprised me most, though, was a scene where a flock of Canada geese flew so close to the camera that you felt you could reach out and touch them. I sat bolt upright, transfixed. How were they able to do that? Who trained the geese. How?

In the film, the geese had followed along behind a boat. If they could be trained to do that, couldn't they be trained to fly with an aircraft?

Early the next morning, I called the producer of the movie for information. He told me the man responsible for teaching the geese in "Skyward" was an experienced animal trainer named Bill Carrick, who had been working with animals for the movies for years, and to my surprise, actually lived nearby.

I called him, and we arranged to meet the next day. It was difficult to concentrate on my work for the rest of the day, I was so excited.

When I arrived at Carrick's nature preserve, he handed me a pair of waders. "Put these on, Bill, and I'll show you around." Before long we were wading through his own wetlands. Wild birds and animals roamed everywhere, but I was particularly intrigued by the elegant Trumpeter Swans. My memories of mom telling me about these unique birds, and their possibility of becoming an endangered species, came flooding back....

I asked Carrick where these swans came from, and he explained: "They were imported from western Canada when they were very young. Native Trumpeters have virtually disappeared from eastern Canada.

We have attempted to re-introduce them here, but it hasn't worked in the wild because they don't have parents who can show them how to fly south for the winter."

After our tour of the preserve, I finally asked Carrick the question foremost in my mind: "Can birds like those I saw in the film "Skyward" be trained to fly with me and my ultralight airplane?"

"I don't see why not. But training isn't quite the right word, conditioning is more appropriate. Actually we condition them to accept us as part of their family. *We* fit into *their* pattern. The technique is called 'imprinting,' and was first described by Konrad Lorenz, the famous animal behaviorist and Pulitzer Prize winner. He discovered that birds hatching out of their eggs become attached to the first living thing they see, which is usually their mother; but it could be any person who fulfills this parental role for them."

"Then you feel it's possible to condition geese to fly behind a small plane."

"Yes, and it's surely worth a try, because if we could do it, it opens up some interesting possibilities."

"You mean like leading the Trumpeters south, as a step-parent?"

Carrick rubbed his chin, thinking. "Might work.... Of course," he advised, "it would be wise to try the plan first with Canada geese before tackling the swans. The swans will present much tougher

technical and environmental problems."

"That makes sense."

"Well, let's start by hatching a gaggle of geese with you present. The goslings should assume that you're their mother, and if they do they'll follow you everywhere. It will take patience, perseverance and time. Keep in mind, though, that whether imprinting these wild birds will ensure their flying with you in the sky is uncertain. It's never been done before."

That was all I needed to hear. It was worth a try!

## Chapter VI

## A New Gaggle

Carrick provided the goose eggs, and when the time came for them to hatch I stood by like an expectant parent. First, little cracks appeared in the shells, and then their tiny beaks peeked out, one by one. Fifteen goslings pecked themselves out of their shells, and started scrambling around. I rounded them up and carefully moved them to their new home, alongside our grass runway.

They didn't seem surprised that their parent was over six feet tall, had a beard, and didn't have wings or a beak. Instead, they happily bumbled around getting used to walking on their tiny legs while I proudly looked on. Clustering around me and inspecting their new world, they couldn't know that they were to be quite different from any other goslings.

Once the goslings had fully accepted me as a parent, my whole family got into the goose raising business. Everyone helped with the care and feeding of our new charges and many family conferences were held on the goslings' behalf.

"What are you going to teach them first, Dad?" Aaron asked.

"We don't really *teach* them anything (remembering what Carrick had said). What we really do is just try to fit into *their* pattern of living. But remember how we saw them fly behind the boat in the movie? Well, we can start by walking up and down the runway pulling a little model plane so they can get used to the idea, and you can help by walking along with them."

"How can we show them how if we can't fly ourselves?"

"Yeah, the plane can't flap its wings," added Geordie.

"Keep in mind, kids, geese are born with certain instincts already built-in, like swimming and flying."

"They're so curious. Look how they peck at everything. And now they're trying to untie daddy's shoelaces."

"They probably think they've got a strange looking mother."

"Well, they must love him, even if he does look weird. Look at the way they trail after him everywhere."

"Okay, you guys, let's head over to the pond and see if they'll swim. I'd love to swim with them."

Well, they beat me to the pond, and frolicked in the water as if they had done it a hundred times before. As my wife Paula and the children watched, the little goslings put on quite a show—cavorting and diving and paddling about, inspecting the lily pads and other plants growing along the bank.

As they clustered together, four year old Carmen commented: "They really love each other, don't they Dad?"

Since the geese followed me everywhere I went, it seemed the right time to get them accustomed to the sound of a noisy engine. If they would follow me while I slowly rode around the runway on a motorbike they might get used to the sound of the engine. The plan was to start this way, and then switch them to following the ultralight plane later.

The first time I started the bike up they scattered as fast as their little webbed feet could carry them. It's surprising how birds that can fly so well can also run so fast. It took a lot of concentration—combined with experienced coaching by Carrick—to train them to trail after me and that scary noise.

Meanwhile, I had to take the new ultralight out for test flights. On one of these first tests the engine failed, just quit, right after take-off, the worst possible time. The engine noise that had frightened the goslings was soothing music to me, and when it suddenly went silent, my heart almost stopped. The end of the runway and a long line of trees was coming up fast.

I got the plane down but with too little room left, and forgetting a basic instruction "never use your feet as brakes," I stuck my feet down. In this feeble attempt to stop, my left foot caught and doubled under the wheel. The entire aircraft flipped up and over and there I was hanging from the seat belt with a broken foot looking at an upside down world.

Even worse, I was now out of action for six weeks, and all hope for working with the geese this year was lost. By the time I'd be ready, they'd be too old and the season too far along. Next year, we would have to start with a whole new gaggle of goslings.

Weeks with my foot in a cast did give me time to re-think the whole project, and come up with a better plan. The most important change was to use an airplane with the propeller at the rear as a pusher, instead of up front as a puller, thus protecting the geese from being sucked into it. The only answer was to re-build my Easy Riser that had been crushed in the collapsed hangar.

## Chapter VII

## C'mon Geese

The following spring, Carrick collected more eggs from nesting geese in his wild life preserve. Fortunately, the geese have a natural back-up system. If they lose their first clutch of eggs they will quickly lay a second set.

I set about rebuilding the Easy Riser.

By mid May the eggs had turned into little cheeping yellow fluff balls. Carmen and I carried them in baskets to their new home down near the pond and runway.

"I'll be getting up every day at sunrise to feed and walk with the geese, Carmen," I said, "and I'll be spending some time getting them accustomed to the sound of the engine. If you want to help before school, you can run up and down the runway with the geese and me.

I have a tape recording we can carry of the engine sounds."

"Let's get started right now, Dad!"

Tremendous patience was required with the geese because they can't be rushed. They had their own timetable. It took many weeks and much help from the family. The more time I spent with them, the more they adopted me as the lead goose, even with my twenty-eight foot wingspan!

To get them used to the aircraft, we took turns pushing it up and down the grass airstrip. They would run along behind, their tiny winglets flapping. Often they would head off in some other direction, usually toward the pond, their favorite place. Since it would be awhile before their wings were large and strong enough for them to fly, they must have decided that swimming was much more fun than learning to fly.

It took all of the will power I had to keep rounding them up, time after time, to try again. The wings of the plane must have seemed gigantic to such young birds.

By the time they developed adult feathers and began to try to fly, I started having doubts that they would ever follow me into the air. During one long week when I had to put the Easy Riser back in the shop to prepare the wings for flight, I was afraid the fast-growing geese, who were now anxious to fly, would forget all about me.

What if they flew off to another life, leaving me behind on the ground, with all the hard work wasted and great expectations ended?

I was not all that certain the plane would perform properly either. My foot still ached, a throbbing reminder of last year's engine failure and accident. And just as the plane became ready, high winds arose that made even taxiing around on the ground impossible. We had to wait. The penned geese were ready, and paced endlessly, flapping their wings, telling me of their frustration at not being able to fly. I could understand, I felt the same way.

At last, the weather cleared.

I climbed into the plane and headed off down the runway, intending to taxi around on the ground first. But it popped into the air before I was completely ready, and when I nervously chopped the throttle, the little plane and I abruptly dropped back to the ground—breaking a piece of landing gear.

Two days later, with repairs made, and having been much more careful in the taxi tests, I became airborne—only to find the rudder wasn't working properly! The plane wallowed all over the sky. In fact flying it was like herding a wayward gosling that had just hatched. With great effort I managed to turn the plane around and land safely.

Brains help, the right tools are important, but after awhile you learn that persistence is vital to get anything worthwhile done. I adjusted the rudder linkage and was finally aloft again.

After half an hour, the old sensation came back and I began to feel at home again in the plane. With the power off it stalled at just over twenty miles per hour, and with full throttle it did forty-five. Perfect. According to my friend Carrick, geese cruise at around forty miles per hour. The Riser had the speed if I needed it, and the plane was now flying beautifully.

So the plane was ready, the geese were ready, and I was ready.

The moment of truth had arrived. The young geese had been

practicing, taking short flights, strengthening their new adult wings. The bugs had been worked out of the plane and my confidence had returned in my flying. But would they follow me? Could we fly together?

Eager for a test flight, I backed the plane up to the goose pen, and Aaron opened the gate. I taxied out to the runway with the geese following faithfully.

My heart racing, I opened the throttle. When I was airborne and it was safe, I looked back expectantly. They were nowhere in sight. I cruised around and finally spotted them back on the ground, near the pool. They wanted to go swimming. Discouraged, I landed and asked Aaron to herd the geese out again.

Once more I took off and looked back. This time the geese took off too, but again they turned around and landed in the pool. My heart sank. I landed, parked the plane, and we put the geese back in the pen. I didn't want to talk about it for the rest of the day.

That evening I called my friend, Murray, and asked him if he wanted to come over the next day with his video camera. I felt sure that this time it was going to work.

He arrived at 6:30 a.m. It was a perfect July morning, brilliant sunshine, not a breath of wind. Murray set up his camera, and Aaron stood by at the goose gate while the rest of the family watched from the balcony of our house.

I taxied up to the pen, revving the engine a couple of times to get the attention of the geese. As they burst out of the gate, I hit the throttle and the plane was airborne in less than 100 feet.

My short runway forced me to pay careful attention on take-off. I needed to make a 90 degree sweep to the left almost as soon as I was airborne, so I couldn't look back until I was leveled out to the north.

As I did, I saw the geese in the air, behind and far below. They seemed to be trying to catch up. I throttled back, slowing down and holding the plane just off stall, flying only fifty feet above the trees. Gradually the geese closed the distance, and suddenly, there they were, alongside!

They were all around me now, a big family flying together! I started a little climb, and they attempted to form up off my left wing, stringing out in a ragged line. They were getting caught in the air currents that spiral off my wing tips, and tumbled around a bit, until the lead goose found the right spot to glide, allowing him to get almost an effortless ride. The rest instinctively arranged themselves behind him in one line of the traditional V formation that all geese fly in.

Executing a long climbing turn I headed back over the house.
My head was swivelling back and forth constantly because I couldn't
take my eyes off the birds. Seeing them up close in their true element
was stunning. I remember one bird especially who dipped down and
slid under my left wing, coming up on the leading edge of the lower
wing, where he found the pressure wave. For a few seconds he just
coasted there, wings outspread, surfing freely near the plane. Then he
slid gradually across to the right, just three feet in front of my face.

It was absolutely thrilling. That one moment was worth all the
years of effort and disappointments. As we passed over the house at
three hundred feet, my family, Murray and Carrick were all jumping
and waving. A great exhilaration swept over me as I realized that we
had *really* done it. These beautiful birds were at last flying with their
big, proud foster parent.

## Chapter VIII

## The Trumpeters

Landing was more exciting than I expected. To lose altitude without gaining speed, the geese pull in one wing and flip down in a tumble, then straighten out some ten feet lower. When they do it together it's really an experience—like falling down with a bunch of acrobatic leaves. As we got close to the ground, the geese resumed a tight formation and glided in with me. We looked like a practiced jet demonstration team.

We were all home safe, and I felt elated as I taxied—and they paraded—over to the cheering crowd of family and friends. When I shut down the engine I was immediately surrounded by the curious geese. It was as if they, too, were excited, and saw this strange man-made contraption in a new light.

They had flown with the parent plane on their maiden flight and now seemed to have a new understanding of it. They proceeded to check the ultralight out—pecking at every little thing they could reach, almost as if they were grooming it.

At every opportunity I had after that I went flying with them, and increasingly we got to be better flyers until we were all able to fly in perfect V formation. In the air, although my craft flew like an awkward kite compared to their beautifully fluid movements, they accepted me and my craft as one of their number. Sometimes I was in back of the V, just one of them with another goose taking the lead. At other times I was the leader.

Each flight was a new experience, a new treat, and always a thrill. We flew all that summer and into the fall.

Sometimes they were so close I could have reached out and touched them. Sometimes I flew above them and looked down at them as we passed over farms and ponds, and I recalled the day long ago when I had sat on that old raft and stared in wonder at that far off flock on its southward journey over my father's farm.

When the snows came and the pond froze, Carrick and I gathered them into the back of my truck and took them back to his sanctuary where they could spend the winter in comfort.

In the spring when I returned to pick them up, they were in one of Carrick's giant netted-over pens among a hundred other geese. I called, "C'mon geese," and out of that huge flock in a great flurry came all my geese gabbling and honking and surrounding me enthusiastically. Within the day we were all flying together again.

Although they didn't know it, they were pioneers in an even bigger adventure that would build on their experience in a very special way. The geese's cousins, the Trumpeter Swans, need a step-parent, someone to show them their old migration route south. People had taken this away from them, maybe we could help give it back.

But that's another story.

And, I hope, my next project. Meanwhile, a boyhood dream that wouldn't die had come true!

## C'mon Geese

Bill's story is captured on the remarkable video, "C'mon Geese." It has won two national awards in the United States and the grand prize at the international film festival on free flight in France.

Copies are available for purchase (home use only) through the following outlets.

In the United States:   The Experimental Aircraft Association
Oshkosh, Wisconsin
Toll free  1-800-843-3612
WI Residents  1-800-236-4800

In Canada:   Paula Lishman Ltd.
Blackstock, Ontario L0B 1B0
(416) 986-5096

Educational Institutions wishing to purchase or rent copies of "C'mon Geese" may contact:

In the United States:   Bullfrog Films Ltd.
Oley, PA 19547
(215) 779-8226

In Canada:   McNabb and Connolly
65 Heward Avenue, Suite 209
Toronto, Ontario M4M 2T5
(416) 462-0223